I0619853

Crowe Press

ISBN: 978-1-939484-55-0

www.crowepress.com

www.martamoranbishop.com

Cover Art Jade Lazlow

This book is dedicated to my sister Helen Diessner and my mother Patricia Moran both of whom worked their entire lives trying to help others have a better life, who struggled and gave all they could without asking for much in return, to Jade Lazlow my soul sister, and to the forgotten in our society.

THE PROPHECY

For fifteen years, the prophecy spread by word of mouth. From mother to daughter, father to son, it spread.

In the dark days of the United States of America, a girl will be born. She will have the power to make people fade from sight. Sound will disappear with a wave of her hand.

She will have the power to control the between times, and during that time, the girl child will call to her all the spirits of the past, present, and future. They will come and join hands with her. Together they will become one power, one body, and that body shall control the magic of the between times. From that day forward, the darkness and despair will disappear from our country. The world will be made new, and all people will once again be equal under the eyes of the law. Kindness will return to our world. Men and women will no longer be the property of the rich.

Corporations will no longer have the power to dictate the lives of their employees, forcing them to remain stuck in a life of drudgery. Money will be made in abundance, but not at the expense of the lives of others. The American dream will return.

DAWN RISES

Book Three of The Divide Series

A dystopian cautionary tale of what we could face
if we don't as a society act to change the outcome.

By

Marta Moran Bishop

PROLOGUE

THE MAN OF THREE FACES, THE PROTECTOR, WHO TEACHES THE ONE WHO IS HOPE!

I am Jamie: The Man of Three Faces: "Ever since Rebecca stood before us beaten, bruised, and announced the Prophecy I started planning and for fifteen years I have been the man of three faces. The dutiful son of one of the richest men in the world, Soucy the man who trades in the lower towns to the uneducated, overworked, poor held near slavery by the rich, and I have planned for the day when the prophecy would happen and the corporations and rich would no longer enslave others. It has taken deception at times, as well as cunning and money that I stole from my inheritance to begin to build a new world outside of the towns, away from the sway and control of the rich.

Some of those whom I enlisted asked me why I did this. My answer was always the same. "If not me who sees the wrong and can help make a better world than who?

Yet, in me was also a connection to Jewell, Rebecca, and Ben's daughter, even though I had not seen her since she was three, still the pull was and is there. I do not know why or what will come of it.

I am Ben: The Protector and Teacher: I had no time to mourn for Rebecca the love of my life, instead, I had a small child that I must protect and guide, teach, and keep safe while she grew and learned, according to Rebecca and her mother Ana she was the Savior from the greed and hate for others that is in this world. Jewell can and does use the Between Times in ways that I would not have believed possible. She can weave cloth that gives the ability to bend light and sound, hiding people from those that would bear them ill.

I toil from dawn to dusk, leaving my little girl in a hovel of a basement apartment that at least keeps her safe. Women are no longer allowed to go out of the house, learn, pray, shop, or meet others, they are at this time property.

However, I sneak books in, and I teach her all that is possible for me to do so in the few hours left to me before I must sleep to go on another day.

I am Jewell: The one who fulfills the Prophecy that my mother died to bring about. The one who brings hope to those who were hopeless.

CHAPTER ONE

Rebecca's silvery fingers still lingered loosely in Jewell's hand. A slight misty feeling caressed her daughter's fingers before she let go.

Turning to the crowd she said. "Fifteen years ago, I stood before many of you and made a prophecy. Today that prophecy has come true. My daughter Jewell has brought us all with her into the between times and opened the door for us to build a new world.

When women were made breeding animals, books were burned, and all but the rich were denied education. Sent to labor in sweat shops, shipped off to fight in yet another war. The poor separated from each other and kept poor and uneducated; it was then our society died.

But we can and will build a new and better one together and the true American dream will spread across the land and the world."

As Jewell reached out to reconnect with her mother, Rebecca seemed to float away and said quietly. "Jewell, not yet." The barest light lit the cavern, not a single sound could be heard, nor did even one of the hundreds filling the vast space move.

As the first rays of the sun started over the horizon, those spirits of the past departed, leaving only Kinnaird waiting near Ana and Rebecca gazing at Ben and Jewell.

Rebecca's long-black hair swirled around her face, her emerald-green eyes moved between her husband and daughter, gazing at them with love and longing. Before turning to the vast crowd waiting.

She threw her arms wide as if to embrace every single person in the cavern and beyond.

"It has begun. The domes and walls are down, no longer is there a separation between the rich and the poor." Her eyes shown with love and pride, that she felt for all those in the room. But your task is not done. You have all gone through so much hardship, your children ripped from you, you have been jailed and put into slavery, and yet there is more to do, and I have little time to explain."

Rebecca's form became a silhouette in the first rays of the early morning sun, as they peeked over the horizon. Her long-black hair moved faster now in the chilly breeze coming off Lake Michigan. Once again, her emerald-green eyes glanced around the room, and then settled on first Ben then Jewell, and finally Ana, her love for them palatable.

Ben, Jewell, and Ana gasped as Rebecca's once nearly solid form began to fade, the light beginning to shine through it.

Ana gripped Jewell's hand and pulled her toward her, whispering in her ear. "In the library behind the books," Ana said with a tremble in her voice and gave the last of her strength to Rebecca as slumped in her seat.

"No grandmother, I'm not ready to lose you. I am just beginning to know you." Jewell said crying.

"Her sacrifices will not be forgotten Jewell, and you will one day meet again. Mother remember you are loved and will be long remembered in the new histories." Rebecca said to the spirit of Ana, as with her hand in Kinnard their spirits faded away.

Rebecca grew just a bit clearer; her form was just a bit more solid. Of all the hundreds of thousands of spirits from the past who had joined them during the between times, only Rebecca was left.

'Jamie, Carolyn, I give you, my blessing. Please come here, you too darling Ben.' They glanced at each other a bit of mystification on Jamie's face, but Carolyn understood Rebecca's blessing and her eyes shone.

Placing a feathery kiss, on Jewell's forehead she whispered Jamie will need you now.' Turning she cupped Ben's face and kissed him. 'My Darling, you must love again.

Flames framed Rebecca's form as it further faded. 'My time here is short. Already I am pulled away as the light rises. You all have little time, to do what you must."

"Hear me, these four will lead you now. My time on this earth is nearly finished, I burned so that Jewell could be safe to learn while she learned how to control the between times." Rebecca said her last words to the crowd.

Except for Kinnaird and Rebecca, the shadowy spirits from the past and future dissipated as the light grew stronger. Kneeling at Ana's feet, Rebecca's shadowy form whispered. "Quickly now, mother it's time."

"Yes!" Was all Ana said, grasping at the mist where Kinnaird stood. A light could be seen flowing from mother to daughter, and as Ana slumped on the bench, Rebecca's form became solid. And for the first time in fifteen years dawns light filled the cavern. The crystals hanging from the ceiling and standing as pillars on the floor glowed with an inner beauty. Their colors mirrored the sunrise in all its glory. Reds, oranges, and yellows played across the faces of the men, women, and children. It didn't matter if they were rich or poor, they all gleamed of gossamer threads made of the finest gems.

Ben, rushed to Rebecca as Jewell held her grandmother in her arms, tears running down her face until she heard Ana's whisper. "The supplies, the supplies are in the library behind the books."

Tears ran down his face, and Ben's arms reached for Rebecca. "I've missed you so much, dear love."

"And I, you. But time is short, and some things must be said.' Looking from Ben to Jewell, and then to Jamie, she said. 'The walls and domes are down across the land, but you have much work to do.

You have all suffered in whispers, feeling helpless in the face of the horror that has been your lives for these last fifteen-plus years. The earth has been ravished; you have all been made slaves of those who would own everything but will never be satisfied with owning as they have black holes instead of hearts. Now you will need to follow Jamie, Ben, and whomever else they choose to lead you. My time is short, and although I love each of you, even those I've never met, I'd like to use the last of my time to say my goodbyes to those I hold dearest."

CHAPTER TWO

Jamie came forward and stood tall, speaking loudly he stated. "Now is the time to rise, across America the word is being spread, and within minutes you must all leave this cavern and march. The corporations, government, and military will shortly be in disarray. But that will not last long.

Some of you may want to take back the cities, you must decide that among yourselves, and it must be decided before anything else is talked of here in this cavern. For if there are those who choose to go into the cities, they must not know where it is we have fled to."

Rebecca interrupted "What is not in the letter I left for you with Ana, Jamie will know." Rebecca turned back to Ben.

"Can you not stay Rebecca, since we have turned back time a bit?" Ben pleaded, tears streaming down his face.

"No darling Ben, I gave my life for you all to have this chance, I cannot have my life back.' The barest of light played across her skin, highlighting her hair with the colors of the rainbow, and the

tiniest of breezes blew strands of it around her
head, a halo of color surrounded her for all to see.

'Because of my sacrifice, I have a bit of time that
was not given to the others.

Time is short, Jamie, Jewell, Ben, Carolyn, Ash,
and Carlos will lead the ones who go out to make a
new life. Jamie and Ash have plans and know the
paths to take. You must decide quickly."

The crowded chamber glistened with color, from
the opening in the ceiling above. 'Ben, Jamie,
Jewell, it is nearly time for us to leave. Mother,
Father is waiting, give them our letters please."

"Yes, Ana said and leaned more heavily on Jewell.
I wish we'd had more time together my darling
girl. But the world changed too quickly, and we
both had our work to do. Remember I love you,
and always will." She whispered as she handed a
stack of papers to Jewell.

The shadow of Kinnaird's hand could be seen on
her shoulder, as her spirit left her body, and joined
his, the two of them young once more, walked
away into the light.

Looking up, Jewell saw the shadowy form of Ana holding tightly to Kinnaird's hand just as their spirits disappeared into the mist.

"Ben my dearest, you must not remain alone for the rest of this lifetime. You still have much to do and need a partner to do it with. Look to Carolyn, she loves you."

"No Rebecca!"

"Yes Ben, it must be. I will be waiting for you on the other side when your time has come. Hurry all of you, make your decisions, there is little time before the army regains control of the city.

As the first rays of the sun started over the horizon, Kinnaird and Ana departed, leaving only Rebecca gazing at Ben and Jewell.

Rebecca's long-black hair swirled around her face, her emerald-green eyes moved between her husband and daughter, gazing at them with love and longing. Before turning to the vast crowd waiting.

A bit shocked, Jamie turned back to the crowd. "For those of you that decide to take back the cities, your fight will be long, and bloody. Oh, not from the richest, for they will hide, they know nothing of survival, but instead, it will come from those who fight for them. The ones that were once called MAGA, were Proud Boys, Three Percenters, QAnon, and The Oath Keepers. That army will want to keep the status quo, they hold most of the guns, and run the war machine. That is what was given to them for their loyalty.

Ana and I were able to get some of the guns, but not many. If you fight you will need to plan carefully, use guerrilla warfare, and pit one against the other.

I do not think now is the time to take back the cities, but I could be wrong, you might win. What I do know is, that it is time to remake our world.

Whatever your choice it must be done quickly before the military regroups. Those who choose to stay, and fight must leave here now, and those who choose the second path must also leave. Know that you may never see each other again.'

Ben and Jamie looked at each other, and out into the crowded room. 'Who among you will stay and fight, and which of you will come with us to rebuild?"

Nathan stepped forward from the shadows of the cavern walls, "before I entered the sewers, I was first in among the Oath Keepers, I still have my old uniform, and can blend in. I will go and fight."

He appeared an unshaven, unclean, underfed, skeleton of a man, yet he pulled himself up to his full height and appeared tall and strong in the morning light. 'I was one of them before I realized what and who they were, and disavowed them, running for quite a while, until I found the sewers. I am ashamed of what I once believed, and I will fight them. Who will join me?"

"I will," Carlos said quietly. 'I want my children to see the beauties of the ancients that are in the museums. Ben, will you watch over Maria and our children? I love them dearly, I don't know if I will make it back to them or you, but I will try."

"No, not you Carlos!" Ben stated plaintively.

"I must Ben, it is my destiny. Oh, I know being a Hispanic I won't fit in, but I'm small and strong. I can hide in the shadows, doing all that is necessary for the cause, and I want to bring back the treasures from the museums so that my children and their children can see them." Carlos said quietly.

There were about a hundred or more, who stood along with Carlos and Nathan, vowing to fight for the city, or to at least create a diversion so that the others could escape. And perhaps save just a bit of the history of the city.

"No Carlos, we have already loaded on the wagons or hidden everything possible that was in the museums this is not your fight, you are needed with us." Said Jamie.

"Are you sure Jamie?" Carlos asked, ready to brave the worst if need be.

"Yes, I am Carlos. Go join Maria and your family please, there will be many who will need both your wisdom, and guidance, to help us all learn each other's language, so we can communicate better with each other."

"I will do as you say, Jamie," Carlos said as he walked through the crowd to stand with Maria.

"Nathan, you will all have the hardest road to follow. Go through the sewers, and out into the city that way. You cannot know where or how the rest of us leave this cavern. By whatever name you call God, may he/she bless you all. Don't forget to hug those you hold dear before you leave, but hurry. We must move out, and close off the cavern, leaving no trace of it for those who will try to find us."

"Jamie, we will do as you ask, this is our path to walk, our fight to fight, we all have much to make up for," Nathan stated, and all those behind him nodded.

As Nathan and his group slid silently out, a few hundred more who had been standing at the fringes of the crowd joined them. Their army was small but determined. Each of them had a cross to bear for their parts in the ending of the world as it had been.

Ben, Jamie, Jewell, and Carolyn stood together, looking at the men leaving the cavern, and headed into the old sewer lines. They had given them what ammunition and weapons they could, but it would be up to those men to find what they needed when they got into the city.

"Will they succeed?" Ben asked Jamie.

"They will buy us time; how many will live is the question. With luck, a few will find us again Ben, but we won't know if they bought us enough time until we are many miles from Chicago, and its suburbs."

"How far away do you believe we will need to be before we can put down our guards just a bit?"

"I don't know Ben, though I believe once we are out of the tunnels and into the forests, we will be able to put down our guards just a little bit, but probably not till at least next year sometime. Those in power won't quit easily. They have always needed a labor force, men for their war machines, and those they can feel superior to."

"That is so sad Jamie, even after all these years in the lower towns, and the take-over of the country, I still had hope for more from even the wealthy."

"Our communities will be built with those ideas Ben. Now I must get everyone back on track or face the chance of failure.

Get the lanterns and torches ready, we will soon lose all electricity down here, just as those in the city will lose theirs." Jamie shouted over those still in the cavern.

CHAPTER THREE

A cool breeze swept through the old freight tunnels, whipping through the cloth of the covered wagons that stretched for miles down the line.

Men in coveralls, jeans, and slacks, some of them obviously poor while others dressed more richly, but they all stood near the wagons.

Some of the buckboards held crates of chickens, some clothing, wood, nails, and household items, two of them carried more fruit trees, and berry bushes, even though many had already been planted years ago on the land they were headed toward. No one knew for sure how far out the settlements would need to go. There were a few buckboards still empty, those they hoped could carry some of the women and children.

"The walls are down, and you can hear the tinkle of glass falling from the domes, it is coming down much quieter than I expected. But that is good, it gives us an extra bit of time that I didn't even dare to hope for.

Pass the word down the line, it is time we get whatever odds and ends that we still need from the city, have the horses arrived yet? "Ash shouted.

"I can see them coming in now Ash." Stated Sam. "Pass it down the line to hitch up horses as they come in. We must be ready to move within the hour. Jamie will be expecting us." Ash stated.

"Will we lose the electricity down here sir?" an elderly white-haired gentleman asked.

"I expect that will happen soon, Jacob. The men working the plants will be leaving them to join us.' Ash said as he stopped one of the younger boys. 'Spread the word down the line to get the torches and lanterns ready, quickly now."

The younger ones had been picked to be runners to keep everyone informed up and down the miles of buckboards and covered wagons. At least until they were moving and some of them rode horseback and could do that job quicker. But while they stood here waiting, it was not practical to use horses for that job.

"Jacob, Jonesy, I'm putting you in charge of finishing the loading and getting the caravan moving.

Stan, and Smitty, come with me. There are things we must do." He said as he moved off and up the tunnel into the upper town, passing the few who were still coming out of the city to join the caravan. Those that had to remain in their positions until the very last minute. Carolyn's women friends are among those, please see that they make it into the tunnels and onto the wagons Stan. Smitty get the powder and bring it to the tunnel entrances. Get it ready so we can blow the tunnels."

"Yes sir!"

There are so very few of the monied people who are a part of this movement. Ash thought. *It is sad, but for so many years they've been raised with such a sense of entitlement, that they will need to learn the hard way. Most will not make it; of that, I am sure.*

Never having had to so much as wash a dish or lift a finger to get their own glass of water from the tap. But instead wasted their time on parties, fancy clothes, and debauchery. Well, no time to dwell on them.

I have the list that Carolyn and Jamie gave me and then I must get out of the town. There is not much time.

At nearly a run, off he went, first to get Carolyn's grandmother's locket, the maps of the tunnels that Jamie had hidden away and headed toward the pet stores.

It will be nice for the children to have small animals to comfort them during the long trip. He thought as he rounded the bend in the road to the pet store, flashlight in hand. "What the heck!" He whispered to himself as he saw a small black cat waiting for him outside the store. "Mew."

"Are you here to help me?" Feeling quite foolish Ash asked the cat.

"Mew." It said again as he opened the door to the store and made his way to the cages, with the black cat at his heels. As each animal leaped out of its cage it followed the small black cat out of the store and toward the tunnels.

"Now I think I've seen everything," Ash said to himself with a shake of his head. Picking up the papers and locket he followed the animals into the tunnels, just as the wind began whipping in from across the water. *The city will wake soon, but not till the sun is up, or the looters enter it, whichever comes first, I guess.*

Ash saw the small coal fires in a few of the higher rooms of the communities, as the first rays of dawn began to rise over the horizon, as he entered the tunnel, leaving the city behind.

He hurried through the tunnels to the caravan, happy to see that all the horses had arrived and were hitched to the wagons. Everything appeared to be loaded and ready.

"We must move out now! All hell will break loose above ground in about an hour. Stoney take this horse and wait here. Smitty will be here with the powder shortly. Blast the entrance as soon as the city is breached by the lower townspeople and then come join us."

"YO!" Stoney stated, taking the horse by the reins, and moving toward the entrance into the city.

Ash mounted his horse quickly; he rode to the front of the caravan. "Move out, follow the wagon in front of you.' He said as he moved past wagon after wagon. 'We have about an hour to reach the caverns if we want to finish loading them, eat and get some rest before we move out again. We will need to be on the other side of these tunnels by sometime tomorrow."

We could feel the pull of the between times even down here. Though I'd have loved to have been in the caverns and to have seen Rebecca again. Still, I know Jamie was right, what we are doing is just as important or maybe even more so. Ash thought as he rode up and down the line of wagons.

CHAPTER FOUR

Jamie moved forward and started taking charge of the crowd. "We need to get organized into groups. One group of men can collect the firewood and begin building cooking fires. Another group can bring up whatever available food supplies. We need a group of women to take charge of the children and babies, and another to begin cooking so that we have food ready when the others get here."

Quickly the men and women formed into groups and began taking care of their assigned chores. Each knew that what they did might mean life or death to the plans. Though each of them did now and then did glance back at Jamie and Jewell, wonder and awe still lit their faces.

"Thank you all, if you have any questions, please feel free to come to ask.' Jamie stated as he walked back over to the others.

"How did it happen, Jamie?" Someone in the crowd yelled.

"Just before the lower towns were built, a plague swept across the world, and the United States was the least prepared of all the civilized countries.

21

Millions died, and the plague helped to cement the separation between the poor and the rich. It along with the already divided country gave more power to the top and the rule of law died.

The little power women still held over themselves was lost, as the men in power demanded that they are made to breed to keep the war machine going.

The divide between the rich and poor became greater, and there were too many who decided to stay home and not vote, write in a candidate, because they had not gotten their wish, in the candidate of their choice, or they voted for a third party to show their disdain for the status quo.

Thus, ended our democracy, the right for people to vote, the rights of women, minorities, and all who were not rich, corporations or oligarchs won.

For we as a nation refused to learn to compromise with our fellow human beings, live with the earth, and protect it and the creatures walking, swimming, and flying upon and over it." Jamie answered.

"What do we do now that the walls are down? Can we rebuild the cities?" Carlos asked.

"Not now, at least not in these cities, maybe our children can. But for now, we must build anew. Someplace where the remains of the government and the troops that are loyal to it cannot find us."

"Do you mean we must hide?"

"Yes, if we had all made other choices before the last real vote was cast, things would have been different. But now even those of us here who were once rich must start again, and perhaps we can learn to compromise and find joy in differences. We once had a chance to clean the air, water, and earth, to stop the never-ending wars against our fellow human beings. To learn none of us is perfect, and to rejoice in what was good, to build better.

"Won't we be able to do that now?" Someone in the crowd asked.

"In a way, but it will be without many of the conveniences we once depended upon. It will be a while before we have electricity, running water, and other such things. We will need to go back to the beginning, and it will be backbreakingly hard work.

We will need to move swiftly, and build more shelters before winter, as some are already built but not enough, I fear. We must learn to help each other as much as possible, and whenever it is needed if we are to survive.

'Carolyn and I must go back into the tunnels for a bit. We won't be long."

"Please be careful Jamie," Jewell said quietly.

CHAPTER FIVE

"What are we to do?" Jewell asked.

"Find the room where Ana hid the supplies and start getting them ready for those that return. For when they get back, we must all make our way out of the cavern, through the tunnels, and into the countryside. We must lead everyone as far from the cities as possible and build shelters, plant crops, and get everyone ready for the coming winter." Ben replied.

"Grandmother told me to go to the library," Jewell stated.

Did she? I must have missed that. I still don't understand why we can't go back into the cities." Ben said.

"Remember what mother said, Father. There will be looting, killing, burning, and destruction, as one group fights another. And I'm sure the large animals that were in the zoo will be loose in the city, there will be no lights, sewer, water, or clean air to breathe. The factories will have stopped, and much will be destroyed.

"How can it be true, what Mother said Father?"

25

"Shush Jewell, I don't have an answer for you yet, but we have so much to do before everyone comes back," Ben said hugging his daughter.

"What do you want us to do Ben?" Carlos asked quietly. His wife and children looked at them all with fear and tremor. For no one knew what the future would hold.

"Come, we must go to Ana's room and find the map that will take us to the place where the supplies are and begin putting them into packs that people can carry."

"Okay my friend, let's get started then."

Jewell led the way to Ana's rooms. "It might not be easy to find the map." She stated.

"I think she will have left us a clue, and we will find it. Take any small mementos that we want too." Ben declared.

Maria and her children looked around them as they walked through the halls behind Ben and Jewell. Their eyes lighted on all the beauty that they found, wishing that they could take it all with them when they left, but at least knowing that they would have the memories to keep with them and to pass on to future generations. "Carlos, it is all so very glorious, isn't it?" She asked.

"Yes, it is Maria, we will remember it all." He said stopping briefly to hug her as they hurried on to catch up to Jewell and Ben.

In the dining room of Ana's home, they first found a stack of bags with a note. "She must have known we would want to take a few things from here."

Dearest Jewell,

The map to the supplies is in a hollow under the rug in my bedroom.

I know you will want a few mementos, but make sure you only take what you will need, for future generations and to build a new life. Also, don't forget to go into the library, on the bottom left shelf there are some readers to help teach those who don't know how to read.

There you will find another letter to be read later when you have all settled outside the cities. Some things happened before the divide that you must know about and teach others.

With that, each of them took a sack of the bags and moved down the hallway. Jewell toward the library and the rest of the group to Ana's room.

Once in the library, Jewell found another letter from her grandmother, which she slipped into a pocket of her bodice, before moving quickly over to the wall of bookcases.

On the left bottom shelf, she located the readers her grandmother had written about, and stopped to browse through a few of the other shelves, picking out a book here and there that might be of importance in the coming days.

There were books on plants, both wild and domestic, and books on the raising of domestic meats and poultry. These she added to her growing stack, along with a few of those books that dealt with all the religions of the past.

After gathering what she found she began putting them carefully into the bags. There are so many here that I should take. She thought. Perhaps, one day I can sneak back and bring some more to the new settlements. But for now, these must-do. It's a good thing that I grew strong from carrying those water pails. She thought as she lifted the heavy bags and draped them across her thin shoulders as if she were Santa Clause of old.

While Jewell was removing books, the others hunted for the map that would lead into the supply chamber.

CHAPTER SIX

Carlos and Maria had collected a small pile of items from the room. A picture of Rebecca, Ben, and Jewell, another of Kinnaird, Ana, and Rebecca when they were young. Combs and brushes, some washcloths, towels, soap, a book on making soap, and an old loam for making cloth.

Carlos and Maria rushed to her side and removed some of the sacks of books, setting them in the pile of things to be taken to the cavern for distribution later. "You found the map, Father."

Looking up briefly, Ben said before reaching into the hollow and pulling out the small black waterproof case he had found. "Yes, and I see you found what Ana wanted you to find and a few more things to boot, daughter." He said laughing.

"I thought we also need books on plants, both wild and domestic, and on animal husbandry along with some on carpentry, though I expect you will be able to teach much about that."

"Perhaps I could teach some things about carpentry Jewell, but there is so much I do not know, I know nothing about building windmills, candle making, or weaving. It is good you thought to bring those. Come here please, you know these caverns a tiny bit better than I do, perhaps you can help me figure out this map."

"Father won't Jamie and Carolyn be of so much more help than I am, they know so much more about the caverns than I do. Perhaps we should take all these things down to the main cavern first. We can study it there, if they come back before we figure it out, they can help."

"That is an excellent idea, Jewell.' Ben said.

'Carlos, Maria do you think the little ones can carry any of these bundles?"

"I think so Ben, they are pretty strong for such young ones," Carlos stated with Maria shyly nodding. Under Maria's direction, the children began packing the bags with the treasures they had found in Ana's room. On top of one of the smaller bags, she placed some sheet music along with a small music box that she had carefully wrapped in one of the cloths and added a few pieces of Ana's more precious jewelry to the bag.

"I don't think we should leave these to possible looters should they find these caverns, or to those of the sewer people who are mentally too far gone after all these years to understand what they have or do anything with them," Maria said quietly.

From the wall, Carlos' young son had taken a guitar that was hanging there and put it over his shoulder.

"Good thinking young man, music is a good thing to bring with us," Ben said to the boy.

Joaquim smiled shyly at Ben's praise and helped his mother redistribute some of the weight of the books into lighter bags for the smaller children to carry.

Four of the children, Carlos, Maria, Ben, and Jewell each shouldered a bag. Maria had taken one of Ana's shawls and made a sack to carry her baby on her hip, almost like a papoose cradle and Joaquim had the precious guitar slung over one shoulder, and a bag over the other. When each was fully loaded and all ready, they took one more look around the room and made their way back down the long halls and into the main cavern.

"Stack them over here," Ben said as he put down his burdens and walked over to the communal table, where he took the map from inside his shirt and spread it on the table.

Maria retrieved some candles from Ana's room and placed them near the map so they could study them better.

"I wonder where Jamie and Carolyn are," Ben said to Carlos. We could sure use their help with this map.

"I'm sure they will be back shortly. They did say something about meeting someone in the tunnels."

"You are right Carlos, let's get on with it."

Jewell and Maria were exploring the large cavern, hoping they might see something that would help them in the quest for the supply room. With each crevice they saw, excitement would build in the room, and everyone would rush over to investigate.

"We cannot keep going on this way, running back and forth between the map and every crevice you find," Ben said.

"Sorry father, Maria and I will try to be a bit quieter in less we really find something of significance."

"Joaquim, please take care of your brothers and sisters for a while, so Jewell and I can look around unhindered."

"Si mother." He stated as he picked up the baby and led his two sisters and younger brother over to a smallish table away from the grownups.

"Should we get on with our search Jewell?" Maria said shyly.

"I guess that would be best Maria, but perhaps I should at least look at the map first. Maybe there is something I saw when I came down here before everyone else that will be helpful in all our searches."

"Si."

The two women walked quietly over to the men. "Father, could I have a look at the map? Perhaps I saw something earlier that will help."

"I hadn't thought of that Jewell, but you could be right. Maybe you did. I know Carlos and I aren't making much headway with it."

Maria walked toward her husband as Carlos reached out and took her hand, he pulled her close to him to comfort her.

"Carlos, what if we can't find it and no one comes who can?" Maria voiced her fears.

Carlos put his arm across her shoulders and spoke. "Not to worry my esposa. Everything will work out; didn't the prophecy already happen?"

"Si, but I can't help worrying marido.' She said laying her head on his shoulder. 'Shouldn't Jamie or Carolyn be back by now?"

"Si."

CHAPTER SEVEN

I'll see you in a bit." Carolyn stated leaving Jamie in the tunnels at the entrance to the city. "Hi Sebastian, I see you have nearly everything loaded on the wagons?"

"We've had most of them loaded for weeks Sir. The men are ready to load whatever is needed from here, we hitched the horses and started as soon as we heard the domes come down, just as you said."

"There is no Sir or master anymore Sebastian, the world has changed. There never really was between us, it was only for looks that you called me that, or at least that is how I considered it. We are friends, who will now go on a new journey together." Jamie said.

"You always have been my friend sir, but what should I call you now?"

"How about you just call me Jamie, as all my other friends do."

"That will be difficult in the beginning, but I will work on it sir, I mean Jamie. Should I instruct the rest to call you Jamie too?"

"Those who know me best yes, the ones I don't yet know well, I'll let you make that decision, but I do know I don't want anyone to ever call me sir again. I must go get the piles of Jewell's tapestries, I do believe we will need them to help hide our passage and our new homes. Besides they are so beautiful."

"I believe you are right Jamie; I hadn't thought about them," Ash stated.

"Now back to work, were the cages opened for the animals?" Jamie finished.

"I left a couple of the zookeepers to open them when everyone that was coming was out of the city, we didn't want the large beasts roaming the city while we were removing things, it would have made things much more difficult wouldn't it? Except for the small animals at the pet stores, those I let out myself."

"Good point," Jamie said.

"Jamie,' Sebastian said quietly, 'if we are friends and I am no longer your servant, would you call me Ash? It is what my other friends and family call me."

"I like that, I certainly will. Now Ash, should we go over the list of what is on the wagons?"

"Good idea Jamie," Ash said smiling ear to ear.

"We've got wood, nails, the large farming equipment, oh not the kind that needs gasoline or oil, but the old-fashioned kind. Shingles for roofs, an enormous amount of cloth, needles, and other sewing equipment. Axes, hammers, saws, coffee, water, sugar, milk, and other handy food supplies, they won't last a large group for more than one winter, and there may be some rationing needed before crops can be harvested. But it will do, and yes, the precious heirloom seeds, a lot of those."

"Did you add the pots and pans that my friends and Carolyn's friends gathered?"

"Yes, as well as a bit of firewood, encase we don't find any on the first leg of our trip."

"Good thinking Ash. It was a great idea to bring the piano, some piano wire, and a few other instruments. Music is good for the spirit."

"I had them put those things on the wagons, Jamie.' Carolyn said as she walked into the tunnel trailed by a small group of women and children.

Some of the women who worked as nannies carried small babies. 'Don't worry Jamie, the babies won't be missed, at least not for a very long time. The mother's seldom visit them, leaving them for weeks at a time with the nannies and they are innocents.' Carolyn said before either man made a fuss.

'Along with bolts of yarn, darning thread, embroidery thread, leatherworking tools, a couple of looms, some extra coffee pots, and a few toys for the children." She continued as if no mention of the babies had ever come up.

"You are so organized Olyn, Jamie said using the nickname he had called her since he was a young boy. 'You always have been. What do you think about taking a couple of dogs and cats with us too?"

"Jamie that is an excellent idea. We should send someone to the pet store quickly and pick out a few. But there must be males and females so they can breed as our society grows."

"Jamie that is already done. In fact, the strangest thing happened when I was opening the pet stores."

"What happened Sebastian?" Carolyn asked.

"Well, this black cat came up and helped. She led all the animals to the tunnels. It was as if she knew exactly what was needed. There she is now." Ash stated pointing toward Sable.

"Oh, my goodness, that is Jewell's cat, Sable.' Stated Carolyn. 'What an odd thing to have happened."

We should be out of here very quickly now. The towns will be waking shortly and not one of us can be here. Oh, they will be busy trying to figure out why there is no electricity or water first, after that they will notice that the walls and domes are down, but if any of us are seen our plans won't work. Jamie said as he turned and led the women and children out of the area.

"Jamie, I've directed Smitty to blow the entrances to the tunnels after we are out of here and then join us."

Sebastian rushed past them to pick his men to open the cages. The innocent must not be made to die of starvation in enclosures, if they were to die, let it be free.

As the last cage was opened, the electricity went out in the city. It had been touchy to open the pens of the large animals, not knowing if they would attack them as they did so, but they had managed. "Come on guys, it will be a bit tricky getting out of here without lights. Did anyone besides me bring a torch?" Adam asked.

"YO!" Came the general shout as the flashlights came on.

CHAPTER EIGHT

Before they had made any headway with the map, Jamie and Carolyn returned to the huge cavern.

"Jamie, Carolyn, first I'm so happy you made it back okay. How are things up in the city?"

"About to get bad Ben. The electricity is out now, the large animals are loose."

"Well, at least I hope you can make better sense of this map than I can," Ben said as he marveled at the crowd that began to enter the cavern and put the bags they carried from the upper town with the others against the wall.

"I believe we can help, but Carolyn will probably be the most help. She was able to sneak down here much more often than I could in these last fifteen years. Father didn't miss her when she was gone, he didn't keep an eye on her as he did on me anyway."

"What were you doing that he would have objected to besides coming into the lower towns?" Ben asked.

"We've been planning this day for nearly fifteen years, Ben. There are wagons loaded with wood and other supplies making their way from the old freight tunnels into the old EL tunnels, though we will need to go back through the sewers where the EL goes above ground until we reach the Howard Street exit. Carolyn and I took a couple of the horses and rode ahead."

"Wagons? What kind of wagons Jamie?"

"Ben it's been mostly, Buckboards, and Covered Wagons. I've had these last fifteen years to put together people, like Ash that I can trust completely. Some of them worked to help me maintain the Soucy character for the lower town market, and some worked in the house, on the landscaping, on my father's yacht, you name it. But for the last ten years, we've been building in the old freight tunnels."

"I wouldn't know where to start to build those types of things, Jamie."

"I didn't at first either Ben, but books are a wonderful thing, aren't they? And I bought horses over the years, Ben. They are pulling the wagons and will help us rebuild. At first, I thought that we'd all just go back and rebuild Chicago and the other cities."

"That is what I thought would happen to Jamie, you could have knocked me over with a straw when Rebecca said we must flee and not go back. How did you know so much sooner?"

"I've been watching and listening in both the lower and upper towns Ben, as well as the political climate. I had a strong feeling that things would get nasty if the prophecy worked and the walls and domes came down."

"I always knew you were brilliant my friend."

"A high IQ is only a tiny bit of help. Mostly you must learn to listen to others. That's when I started gathering products and people to build. The next step was to locate places we could all go to, though I must admit I had no idea it would be in the thousands."

"I hadn't counted on that either Jamie. But for now, we need to find the supply cavern." Ben said.

Carolyn and Jewell were pouring over the map. "I know where the room is," Carolyn said loudly.

Ben, Carlos, and Jamie rushed over to the table.

"See this mark!!"

"YES, but what does it mean?"

"This is Ana's house. There is a secret door in the library behind the bookshelves."

"Of course, I should have realized that is what she meant when she told me to look in the library before she died.' Jewell said, as they all turned and rushed back to Ana's house and into the library. 'She was very clever, wasn't she?"

"That she was Jewell, and she had a very long time to get it built too," Jamie stated as he began pulling on bookshelves.

CHAPTER NINE

"Over here!!!" Yelled Ben, as he pulled a book out and the wall opened.

Stacked from floor to ceiling were supplies, cradles, old ringer washing machines, clothesline, rope, copper wire, cloth, winter coats, and boots along with sturdy warmer weather footwear. There even seemed to be plans for building windmills and solar panels, along with materials that could be used, and to everyone's surprise, was a stack of huge camouflage netting.

"My God! I didn't think of so much of these things.' Jamie said with shock in his voice 'She must have suspected there would be more than we'd thought were coming."

"But camouflage netting, why would we need that, Jamie?"

"The only thing I can think of is that after a few weeks when things calm down a bit, and so many are dead, the government will send out its troops, including drones, helicopters, and airplanes, why they may even use the space satellites to attempt to find and punish anyone who got away."

"Do you think it will get that bad Jamie?" Ben asked worriedly.

"To tell you the truth, I don't know. I don't suspect Ana knew either but covered her bases in case. I think we need to do so too. When we get settled, the first thing will be to put up the netting."

"I guess we will be better safe than sorry Jamie," Ben replied.

"All I know is I don't want to take a chance with everyone's lives by not being prepared for the worst," Jamie answered.

"Me neither."

Jewell, Carlos, and Carolyn were inspecting the supplies in the cavern as they listened to the conversation between Ben and Jamie. "Well guys, we best get on with it, there is no going back now.' Carolyn stated flatly. 'Jamie, when do you think Ash and the others will reach near enough for us all to begin loading?"

"Sis, they would have traveled faster than we could have in the old freight tunnels and sewers if we were walking. I suspect they will be here within the hour."

"Maria and I can go out to the main cavern and see who is able to come help, they are smaller and less able to help move all this heavy stuff out of here."

"Brilliant, thank you, Jewell.' Said Jamie quietly. 'Don't forget to take Sable with you.' He said with a smile. 'That cat appears to have a way of being in two places at once."

"I hadn't noticed that, but it makes sense. Though I can tell you she'd follow me even if I tried to leave her behind." Jewell said with a twinkle in her voice, as the two women turned around and left Ana's house.

CHAPTER TEN

Entering the large main cavern Jewell and Maria found it overflowing with men, women, and children. Maria rushed over to her five little ones to make sure they were okay. "How are you all doing Joaquim?" She asked her oldest son.

"All's okay mama. We met some nice people who've been helping with Rosa." Joaquim said with a smile. Mama this is Sarah, she has two little ones of her own."

"Hi, Sarah.' Maria said shyly. 'Thank you for helping my children. Jewell, have you met Sarah?"

"No Maria, it's my pleasure to meet you, Sarah."

"Oh no, it is my pleasure. I just don't understand why we can't go back into the city and what is going to happen now. Do you know Jewell?"

"Yes. But we need to tell everyone at once. We must get organized quickly.' Terrified of the crowd, Jewell locked eyes with one of the young women she had met before, as she answered Sarah. 'Isn't that Mabel?" Jewell said loudly.

"Yes, Jewell.' Mabel, the homely young woman with patched clothes responded. 'What can I do to help."

"Please can you go get Jamie? He's in Ana's library. I can't do this alone; I don't know what to tell all these people."

With a brief nod, Mabel ran off toward Ana's home.

As Sarah watched Mable run toward Ana's dwelling, she said. "I'll go ring the bell, that will get everyone's attention quickly, Maria will you watch my little ones for a bit?" Sarah said as she rushed off, knowing that Maria would.

The ringing of the bell sounded deafening to Jewell, as she stood by herself trembling and praying that Jamie would hurry up. *With luck, I won't have long to wait. He'll know what to say, though I wonder at myself for automatically thinking of Jamie and not Father or Catherine.* She thought.

Jamie with Ash at his side, and Mabel following hurried toward Jewell. "She looks terrified Ash, I suppose it is no wonder, she has never spoken to anyone but Ben up until a few days ago."

"You'll both know what to do Jamie," Ash replied as they reached the dais where Jewell was standing. The bells had stopped ringing and a huge crowd of men, women, and children stood staring at Jewell.

"Oh, Jamie thank you." Her voice trembling with pent-up emotions.

As he reached her side, he looked into her eyes, his fingers sliding down the side of her face and across her mouth, teasing the bottom lip softly. Startled he caught himself. *I didn't know*. He thought stunned at his own actions.

Ash looked at the two of them, with a knowing look, but said nothing as he waited.

Jamie softly took Jewell's hand in his and the two of them turned to face the crowd.

"What's happening Sir?" A short-skinny man of mixed race yelled, and a groan of agreement filled the room as people looked at one another with fear and hope.

"Some of you know me as Soucy, from the market, others who lived in the upper town know me by Jamie. I don't have time to explain all of that now but promise I will do so as we travel or when we get to where we are going."

"Where are we going? I don't understand why Rebecca said we couldn't go into either the city or the lower town." Yelled a tall man with a pockmarked face. His clothes were so patched that it was a wonder they stayed on his body.

"That is also something that will need to wait for an explanation I'm afraid. There is no time for that either. Again, I promise you will understand as we go. Please bear with us, we need your help desperately now and we have very little time.' Though he knew the mood of the room had settled down, Jamie had trouble focusing on what he knew needed to be said.

The softness of Jewell's hand lit a fire deep inside him, and it continued to keep his mind occupied, try as he might. 'Ash, would you please explain what we need help with." Jamie said turning to his friend, a blush spreading across his freckled face.

Ash took a step forward. "Jamie and I have known each other for over fifteen years. During this time, we have collected supplies, and horses, built wagons, and Jamie has bought the land. Enough land for everyone to settle comfortably on and build a future.

The wagons are traveling through the old freight and sewer tunnels."

"What tunnels." Could be heard from the throng of people.

"I know many of you did not know that these tunnels existed and in fact neither did Jamie and I before we began our research. Let it suffice, for now, to know they are there and soon the wagons will reach us."

"Ana, many of you just knew her as the old mother, also compiled a huge supply of things we will need in the coming years. Some of those things, such as coats and shoes, will need to get distributed now, I fear there will not be enough coats to go around, so some may need to make do with blankets until more coats can be made, which we can start sewing while traveling. The rest of the supplies will need to be carried down to be ready to load onto the wagons the minute they get here." Jamie piped in.

"We do not have much time. We need the women to organize themselves, some will take care of the children, others will cook meals for everyone, and the rest of you, distribute the clothes that are in storage." Jewell said holding firmly to Jamie's hand.

CHAPTER ELEVEN

"I need every able-bodied man to come with us and begin to carry the supplies down here so they are ready to load on the wagons. As near as Jamie and I can figure we have one day to be loaded and two more to be out of the city and on our way before the Army begins looking for us." Ash said getting a nod from Jamie.

"You mean we have only three days to be completely out of the city and the tunnels?" A smartly dressed businessman stated. It was obvious to all that he had grown up in the upper town.

"I'm afraid so Alfred," Jamie answered.

"Why so little time Jamie?"

"The nearest we have been able to calculate is that the worst of the carnage and looting will be over in three days, the army will have arrived to take care of anyone still causing a commotion. It will be after that that they will begin looking in the lower towns. Those in power are not going to like the loss of profits from the factories and the labor camps. Nor will they appreciate the walls and domes being down, the city beginning to flood and the rich in the upper town having to drink the same water and breathe the same bad air that those in the lower towns have lived with for fifteen years." Jamie replied.

"I expect you are right on that Jamie. Is that all the time we will have to get far enough away?" Alfred replied.

"No, it will probably take the soldiers at least a few days to cover all the lower towns and find these caverns. We plan on blowing up the entrances when we leave, so with luck, they will not find them at all. After that, they start to spread out into the countryside."

Just as Jamie finished his statement, the earth shook, and a horribly loud crash could be heard.

"What was that?" A woman screamed.

"I believe that the entrance to the tunnel was just blown up. There is no going back now, except through the sewers, and those will be blown as soon as Nathan's group gets through them." Ash stated calmly.

"When do you believe they will bring in the tanks and planes, Jamie?" Stewart asked.

"Frankly, I don't believe those will be called in for at least a week, if at all. As much as they will want desperately to find us. Gasoline has been in short supply for years now, what with all that has been used in the continual wars. But if they do, it will be a last resort and short-lived."

"How fast will the wagons carry us?" Alfred asked.

"I'd like an answer to that too." Said Stewart.

"If we travel at a decent pace, we should be able to cover ten to twenty miles a day. If we are in the tunnels and sewer lines, we can travel during the day. However, there will be places where we will have to get out of the wagons and pull the horses up between the sewers and tunnels. But as soon as we hit the outskirts and go above ground, we will have to do all our traveling at night and hide as best we can during the day." Ash answered.

"After we leave the freight lines and go through the sewers to the Howard Street EL there, we will climb above ground. It should take us approximately two days. With luck that will include the time loading and getting out of these caverns." Jamie added.

"So according to what you have figured out, we should be just about a hundred miles north of what used to be Kenilworth Wisconsin. Stated Jonesy an elderly man, who appeared to have had too many hard years under his belt."

"That is what we are figuring. We will be branching off to the northwest when we exit the EL. Our caravans must split up into five or six groups. Each group will get enough provisions to make it to Kenilworth and from there we will join up until we reach our destination and start building. In the beginning, smaller groups will make it less obvious for anyone looking for us when we are still so close to the city.' Jamie stated. 'What is your name sir, you seem to know that area a bit."

"Jonesy, sir, and yes I was brought up in Kenilworth before the divide happened, and they rounded us all up."

"Jonesy, I'd like it if you would work with Ash on routes from there. I bought quite a land farther north, northwest, and west of Kenilworth. I have men that I trust already building out there. But we need to get all of us to the areas."

"Yes sir, I'd be happy to help," Jonesy said standing up taller than he had in over fifteen years.

"Now, we've answered all the questions we have time for right now. Jewell, will you take charge of delegating which women will do what?"

"Yes, Jamie.' She said her green eyes meeting his for the second time and blushing. 'Maria, and Mabel, will you help me? Ellen,' Jewell yelled as she spotted Ana's servant. Can you help us with this too? You know so many of the women here."

Ellen, Mabel, and Maria rushed to join Jewell, as she released Jamie's hand, she looked at him with a blush that spread across her cheeks. A small smile lit Jamie's face as he brushed her cheek with his long slender fingers again before he turned to leave with Ash and Jonesy in tow, calling the rest of the men to follow them.

"Jewell, Sarah will be able to help Mabel gather the women that will watch over the children. I don't know any of them or I'd take on that job." Maria said quietly.

"Ellen, will you help Maria to divide the rest of the women into those that will cook and those that will distribute supplies? I am going to go back to the library and begin dividing up those supplies that will be distributed today." Jewell said with a newfound strength that she didn't know she had.

CHAPTER TWELVE

"Ladies, Ellen, and Maria will decide who is to cook and who is to divide up the supplies that I send back. Sarah and Mabel will help get those of you who will oversee the children for the next day or two settled. Does anyone have any questions before I leave to go divide supplies that we need now from those to be loaded into the wagons?" Jewell asked.

Silence met her question, each woman looked toward the group that they felt they'd best fit into.

As the women watched the last of the men tromp down the walkway toward Ana's dwelling, they sighed and moved toward either Ellen and Maria or Mabel and Sarah. They were on a mission and knew time was of the essence. It didn't matter if their clothes were patched or they had diamonds in their ears, they had a job to do and knew it.

Before long the children were in small groups with one or more women watching over them and trying to keep them occupied with small games and stories. Pots were pulled out and put near the outdoor wood stoves, and an assembly line of women cut carrots, onions, garlic, potatoes, leeks, and a variety of other vegetables along with chunks of meat, while others gathered water, started fires in the stoves and began to roll out dough for bread.

Not an idle hand in the room, nor did it remain silent as women chatted with each other as they cooked, cut wood, or played with the young ones. Every so often a mother would stop and go over to scold or cuddle her own child if it appeared to become frightened or unruly, but that seldom happened.

"Mabel, Jewell seems to have grown up, overnight, doesn't she?' Ellen asked. I mean she seems so much older than she was just yesterday."

"I noticed that too Mabel. I think in part it is her channeling the Between Times for us all, but perhaps she also gets some strength from that young red-headed man of hers."

"I did notice that it will be interesting to watch them as time goes on. I do believe, regardless of their feelings toward each other, it will take them a bit of time to sort through it." Mabel replied, a small smile lit her homely face, making it light up and giving it a beauty all its own. One that no one had noticed before.

"Do you think he will believe her too young for him, no matter how he feels about her?" Ellen asked curiously.

"That could be, but still, I don't believe she will stand for that too long. As shy as she is there is a tremendous strength of spirit in her. I don't believe even Jamie will be able to stop what will be."

"Didn't Rebecca give Jamie her permission before she departed back into the world of spirit?" Ellen asked.

"I remember that. Though he looked quite confused at the time. It is all going to be so interesting, especially for us women. I mean we have never had a chance to meet each other, let alone had the opportunity to be courted. I wonder what it will be like to have a man come calling?" Mabel said with a twinkle in her eyes.

"Humm, I hadn't had time to think of that. Oh, here comes Jewell, Carolyn, and a group of men carrying bags of items. I guess it is now time to start divvying up things. I wonder what there is, besides clothes.' Ellen said as she saw a couple of small puppies run toward the children. 'I guess that answers a part of my question."

Jewell and Carolyn began directing the men to place things into separate stacks.

"Stack the adult coats over here, and the children's next to them. Use this space for the shoes, and boots, separating them according to children or adults. And the same with the shirts, pants, underwear, dresses, and scarves.'

"Jewell, there won't be enough coats for all the children," Carolyn stated matter-of-factly.

"The littlest will have to make do with blankets, and even some of the adults might too, at least until we can make more coats," Jewell replied.

'All of the toys will go here." Carolyn directed the men. *There wasn't a huge number of toys, they would have to be shared, but what was there would help please the little ones and give them something to do as their mothers worked.*

CHAPTER THIRTEEN

A chorus of voices could be heard yelling. "The wagons are coming."

"God that smells good" Jacob, one of the younger men stated hungrily.

"I do believe at least there is coffee ready Jacob, and you all deserve a cup before you go back to help carry the rest down to the wagons. We will eat when the wagons are loaded." Carolyn stated.

"Jewell, do you see how Jacob looks at Mabel? I think it is very cute."

"Truthfully I've been so busy I hadn't noticed much yet, but I'll be mindful now Carolyn."

"Please Jewell, call me OLyn, I much prefer it and it is what you called me as a baby."

"Did I really, it is so long ago, I had forgotten, but I will from now on. Though to be truthful it might take a bit getting used to, especially if you marry Father."

"Goodness, whatever gave you that idea Jewell?"

"I've seen the way you look at him, and I heard my mother giving you the blessing. I think I also have a bit of my grandmother's second site, at least where you and father are concerned."

"Do you think that Ben will ever allow himself to love another?"

"One day he will, just be yourself and have some patience. Now on with the task at hand. It won't be long before we have many mouths to feed and get bedded down for the day."

Jamie walked into the cavern and stated loudly. 'We will move out before nightfall. We need to finish loading, eat, and get a bit of rest before then." He said as he began helping to load the wagons."

A groan went up from the crowd, but they continued loading.

"And as we both know what Jamie wants, Jamie gets," Carolyn said with a chuckle.

"Or at least he thinks he does. We will see about that as time goes on. He has some ideas that just won't suit me at all." Jewell stated as the two women moved off to start helping with the distribution of clothing.

"Only one pair of shoes, and one pair of boots per person or child. I'm sorry, the babies will need to be carried, there are no baby shoes, but there are plenty of warm blankets to wrap them in and wool socks for their tiny feet." OLyn called out.

"Clothing is in short supply, there are many more here than anyone expected, so divide it up as equally as possible. No one should be without, we will be going into some cold weather soon and will like to spend some time outside in the snow and icy conditions, especially when we are traveling at night.' Jewell added. 'But on a good note, there is a large supply of cloth, leather goods, looms, yarn, and other things that will enable us to make clothes before it is time to sheer sheep." Jewell added.

"When do you think we will be loading the children onto the wagons?" Raegan, a tall thin blonde asked.

"I expect we will do that before dark. From what we could tell, the men had well emptied Ana's storage already, and I expect Ash and Jamie's men have most of it all loaded already.' OLyn answered. 'How is food coming ladies?"

"We could feed the women and children now, and bed down the little ones. So that the women could help serve the men right away." Sarah answered.

"Thank you let's get started. We can't afford delays and the men will be very hungry."

By the time all the women and children had eaten, and the children slept side by side along one wall, the men began rushing into the hall.

There wasn't one of them that didn't feel a hole in their belly the size of a basketball.

CHAPTER FOURTEEN

Ben, Jamie, Ash, and Jonesy poured over the map of the old freight, sewer, and EL tunnels, laid out on the large table in Ana's dining room.

The tapestry hanging on the walls in the room glistened, lit by the many lanterns placed on the wood table, to enable them to see the small markings better.

Some of the freight tunnels are still in use, or they were up until last night, to bring supplies into the city. When the troops are called in to stop the worst of the looting and killing, after the city is secured, they will turn to look for those missing from the lower towns. The freight tunnels will be the first breached.

We need to get through the freight tunnels quickly and move into the sewer tunnels and we will need to watch for the sewer people though I believe most have probably gone up to loot the upper town."

"Jamie, won't they see the ruts from the wagons and horses in the tunnels and follow them?' Ben asked. 'Perhaps we could have a few men follow behind and cover the tracks."

"Great idea Ben, Jonesy would you pick about a dozen men for that job?"

"I'll get right on it. Sir, from what I remember of the old sewers and from there to the EL at Howard Street, once we get in there it will be nigh on impossible for anyone to trace us." He said as he turned to leave the room.

"Jonesy before you go, please take Ash with you. Ash, please bring Jack back with you. You know the guy that used to work for my father doing the blasting for the strip mines before I recruited him?"

"Sure Jamie, but out of curiosity why?"

"We will need someone to lay some small charges behind the cavern tunnels to prevent anyone from finding this underground city. Just enough to stop a search, but not so much as to stop us from coming back if we need to."

"Ah yes, I see the need for that. I'll get him. We must make sure no trace of the wagons, or horses that entered the sewers or the people that have been living down here for years remains for anyone to find. Blowing a few rocks in front of the entrances is a great way to start. I believe Jack is still down with the horses." Ash replied as he and Jonesy left the room.

"Jamie, I'd recommend we hang some of Jewell's tapestries on the inside of both the entrances to these caverns as well as the entrance between the freight and sewage tunnels too."

"Again, another great idea Ben, that way anyone coming in from our side would be able to find them, but they'd help hide the entrances from those looking for us from the city side."

"Won't the blasting powder cause too much noise in the upper town Jamie?"

"Not if we do it at the height of the rioting."

"Good point."

"Don't let looks deceive you, Ben, Jack may look old, but he is very spry and knows powder."

"Jamie, it is hard to fathom how much time you have all spent planning this, all the while I was in the lower town going to work and just trying to keep Jewell safe."

Jamie's look softened with the mention of Jewell's name. "I've had fifteen years, though the first five were mostly taken up with recruiting those I could trust, research, and of course keeping my father in the dark about my activities. Sometimes that was hard. Like the time I had to convince him to let me have the land that he bought to drill on."

"How much land is it?"

"Well, all told probably a hundred thousand acres, but it is spread out over several states."

"However, did you convince him? From what I remember of your father that couldn't have been easy."

"You are right, it wasn't. It took some doing to get him to believe that we'd make more of a profit waiting until the country was nearly out of natural resources before we began the projects. I was just stalling, waiting for the prophecy, and building up my own little band of men, who would go and plant trees and start building a bit, though I had no idea we'd need to house so many people.

I fear most of us will be spending much of the year in the wagons, while we build more dwellings. Ben, we all know the plan, I'm going to wait here for Ash and Jack. I want to go over locations for the blasting powder with Jack and make sure he has a way out and knows where to find us. You should go get some food and rest. Oh, and if you could persuade someone to bring some food and coffee in here it would be greatly appreciated.

Luckily, we already planted most of the fruit trees, and berry bushes, so at least we should have that to eat before winter sets in."

"Will do Jamie, but before I rest, I want to talk with Jewell and Carolyn about having the tapestries taken down from here and ready to go up in front of entrances. Also, I think Jewell needs to start teaching some of the women to use the between times. We will need to do more than put camouflage over the wagons as we travel.

The camouflage and tapestries will need to hide the villages for quite some time to come."

"Agreed," Jamie said nodding at Ben. *Boy am I exhausted, and we aren't even on our way yet!* Jamie thought as he slumped down into one of the chairs, laying his head on the table as he waited.

CHAPTER FIFTEEN

Ben marveled at the beauty of the stalactites and stalagmites as he left Ana's dwelling. The light from the various cooking fires lit them from within. I wish I had a camera; it is so beautiful, and I'd love to share it with my grandchildren someday. But that is not to be, perhaps someday we can make a trip back here. He thought as he walked through the throngs of people, some sat eating in small groups, and others were still in line for their meals. Finally, he spied Jewell and Carolyn sitting alone eating with their heads close together talking. So close did they sit that Jewell's black hair and Carolyn's blonde strands mingled together.

They are both such beautiful women Ben thought. I guess in a way, I do love them both, though not in the same way that I love Rebecca. I don't believe I will ever feel that no matter what Rebecca said.

Nearly simultaneously both women looked up as they saw Ben's shadow coming toward them.

"Father, you must be starved," Jewell said as both women jumped to their feet. A blush spread over Carolyn's face as she looked up at Ben.

"I'll get something presently Jewell, right now I need you to listen to me. On the trip, you must teach some of the women to work with the between times, so that we can hide our passage from prying eyes. It will take more than just you to do this, I am sure."

"I don't know how to teach it, Father."

"You will have a day or so to think about a way, but you must do it. Also, we need you and Carolyn to strip all your tapestries from the cavern and Ana's dwelling. Most of them must be hung in front of any entrance into this area, though we will need to save most of them to hide other things later."

"Okay Ben, I'll get started on that immediately stated Carolyn.

"Carolyn, someone must take some food and coffee to Jamie he is in the dining room at Ana's."

"I will do that father," Jewell said a blush slowly swept up her face, as she turned to go to get a tray.

"Have you eaten Carolyn?" Ben asked.

"Not yet, I was waiting till those who have been working the hardest got their food." She replied, a blush creeping up her face.

"Why don't we both go get in line," Ben said as he looked around the huge cavern, the youngest children were lying wrapped in blankets against one of the far walls, and it almost appeared as if Sable was directing the puppies and kittens as to which children would need them most to cuddle with. *A small smile lit his face as he remembered a young Jewell with Sable firmly in her grasp as she slept in the small room in the lower town.*

There is just so much left to do, Ben thought as he moved into line to get some food. *I don't see how we will manage, no matter how organized Jamie and Ash are. I feel so useless, without any knowledge or ability to help right now. Well hopefully, I'll learn what I can do later.* So deep in thought, Ben didn't notice Carlos walking up to him until he spoke.

"Ben, Carolyn, I have some food set up over there for you. I have been waiting and knew you would be hungry."

"Carlos, you startled me. But it is nice to see you and thank you. I am hungry and I am sure Carolyn is too." He said as they stepped out of line and followed his friend across the room. As they walked Ben chatted with Carlos and looked around the huge cavern. *There are so many people. I just wonder how we are going to move them all. But I'm sure there will be a plan in place soon if there isn't already.*

Carolyn walked ahead of the two men, eager to visit with Maria and the children. *A bit of peace and joy is just what I need after everything that has happened in the last twenty or so hours, and we haven't even started on our trek yet.*

Ben watched her walking. *I've never thought of Carolyn the way that Rebecca said I will.* He thought. *Nor did I have any idea that she loved me. Yet, there is a grace in her movements I hadn't noticed before. Perhaps, as time goes by….*

CHAPTER SIXTEEN

All the way back to the library with the platter of meats, cheese, potatoes, green beans, and coffee, Jewell couldn't keep her mind off Jamie. *Yes, I did feel a spark pass between us in the cavern, and when he touched me, it was as if fire went through my veins, but marriage, that I hadn't considered. Nor am I aware if he felt what I did when we touched. How does one know what someone else feels?* Jewell wondered.

Lucky for her, the door to the library was cracked open when she reached it, and all she had to do was push it a bit with her foot, to open it enough to get in with the platter. *He's sleeping, I think.* She thought.

The sound of the door banging open startled Jamie out of his slumber. *I hadn't realized I was so tired,* he thought looking up to find Jewell in the doorway with a tray laden so heavily with food that it could have served six full-grown men.

A blush crept up his fair skin, till it made his red hair appear even darker. "Hi, Jewell. Here let me help you." He said jumping up from his chair and nearly spilling it on the floor in his hurry to get to her.

"Slow down Jamie, you're likely to trip on something, and it will make me start laughing. If I do, I make no promises about what will happen to this tray." She said with a smile creeping up to her eyes. *Maybe that's how you tell if someone thinks of you the way you think of them.* She thought happier than she ever remembered being.

Though her next thought sent her spirits down again. *Perhaps he's just being polite. What is wrong with me? I can't seem to keep my mood in one place.*

God, she is so beautiful. Jamie thought as he reached her side and took the tray from her hands. "You will eat some of this with me, won't you? There is enough here for an army." *I don't even remember feeling this jittery when I was just a kid with a crush on Rebecca. I wonder if it is only because of what Rebecca said about Jewell and me getting married and having children.*

As he placed the huge tray on the gleaming wood table Jamie thought. What do I say to her? I wonder if Ben felt this way when he first met Becca?

"Would you pass the meat, Jamie?" Jewell asked politely. Eager to say more, but that is all that she could get out.

"Of course, do you want some potatoes and gravy too Jewell?" Jamie replied. *God, I'm acting like a complete fool.*

"Yes please.' She replied. 'Jamie, about what my mother said."

"We can talk about that later Jewell. I don't think now's the time, do you?"

"It's as good a time to start the conversation as any Jamie." She said a blush creeping up her face at her newfound courage.

Just in time, the door burst open. Ash entered with Jonesy and Jack in tow. "Oh, thank goodness, food. I think we could all have started eating the horses about now."

"Jewell brought enough for all of us and a few more," Jamie said with a sigh of relief. *I'm not ready to have the conversation Jewell wants yet. Thank goodness Ash, Jonesy, and Jack came when they did.*

Damn! What bad timing. Jewell thought with a small smile for the men. "Come on and take a seat. I'll get the coffee."

"Coffee would be wonderful," Jonesy said as he loaded his plate with meat, cheese, potatoes, and gravy, careful to leave the vegetables off his plate.

"All the wagons are loaded. The rest of the men are eating or about to eat. I figure we don't have enough room in the wagons for everyone to ride Jamie." Ash said with a mouthful of food.

"We'll have to take turns. We'd have to anyway, as we'll need to alternate the men sleeping and eating.' Jamie replied. 'How many do you think will need to walk?"

"We figure from the crowd we have about half will need to be walking. We can alternate them. But only the babies, small children, and elderly or sick, will always ride in the wagons. The rest will have to take their turns walking beside the wagons." Jonesy replied.

"Smitty blew the freight tunnel entrances in the city and has joined us. He said that all hell has broken loose in the city. We need to start moving out quickly." Jack added.

"How long do we have?' Jamie asked. 'Everyone is pretty exhausted."

"I expect those who have eaten should take an hour's nap, those who are eating should finish. They can have the first shift riding in the wagons and get a few hours sleep before switching places with those who only had an hour." Ash said.

"So short a time? I had been counting on giving them at least a day." Jamie asked.

"We don't have that much time Jamie, I'm afraid an hour is all we can give them. We must be in the sewage tunnels before dark." Ash replied.

"We must leave while it is still noisy enough in the city to blow the entrance." Jack piped in; his mouth so full of food one could hardly understand him.

"I see. Jewell, would you go up and get those who have eaten to pack up and lie down for an hour? Please explain that we must load in one hour and everyone will need to take a turn walking all the way to our destinations."

"They won't be happy Jamie, but I'll make clear what's at stake to them all," Jewell said, leaving the room at nearly a run.

CHAPTER SEVENTEEN

Jewell entered the cavern, spying her father sitting with Carlos, Maria, and Carolyn she first went to them.

"Father, we must move out in an hour. Do you know if everyone has already eaten?" She said looking at the men still in the food line.

"I believe they are looking for second helpings Jewell." Maria piped in.

"An hour? Everyone's exhausted, except maybe the little ones who are sleeping over by the wall." Ben said pointing at the children rolled in blankets against one wall.

"It's worse than that father. Everyone except the youngest, oldest, and those that are ill will have to take turns walking. No one expected quite so many people and there aren't enough wagons."

Jamie stood on one of the tables. "Listen up folks, we don't have enough room in the wagons, or buckboards for all to ride, nor do we have enough horses. Those who ride best and are strongest among us must carry the poles to hold up the netting. Only the old, sick, and the youngest children will ride all the time. The others will take turns, walking alongside the wagons, and buckboards. If you are near the buckboard where the caged chickens are you will need to keep them always covered, except when we are far enough out of the city, and under a canopy of trees. The elderly and women will drive the wagons, and the buckboards."

"Jamie, we didn't sign up for this, we are from the upper town, and none of us have spent hours walking."

"I understand Jason, but there are not enough wagons, and the able-bodied are going to have to walk, along with pulling their share on the road, and when we reach the settlements, that is the way it will be from now on. No one is better than another now. Do you all understand?"

With much grumbling and conferring among their groups, Jason finally acknowledged the new reality, as did the rest of the group. "I guess we had best take off our finery folks, ladies break off your heels, or find some other shoes. You can't walk miles in those." He said pointing at his wife.

"I can take the first shift.' Said Carlos, 'but I don't think anyone will be happy about this."

"No, Carlos they already aren't. Did you hear the discussion that Jamie just had with the group from the upper town?' said Ben. "Did anyone say why only one hour Jewell?"

"Yes Father, Jack rode back from blowing the entrance to the city and told us that all hell had broken loose up there. Ash and Jonesy said we must reach the sewage tunnels before dark so we can blow that entrance before the noise dies down."

"That makes sense, though it's good days walk to the sewage entrance. God, how are we to tell these exhausted people?"

"It is their lives that are at stake Father," Jewell answered.

CHAPTER EIGHTEEN

"Throw those camouflage netting over the wagons. Everyone on horseback must take a pole to hold up the netting over the animals, anyone walking will need to keep very close or under the netting," Jack shouted to the crowd.

"Are we expecting to be spied on from the air?" Carlos asked.

"Don't forget the satellites, even though the military won't be able to start out looking for us, we don't need someone to look back at the satellite images."

"That is a brilliant idea.' Jamie stated. 'Get to it, folks. I would never have thought of it Jack, thank you."

"We must break the caravan into smaller groups, just enough to not appear as if we are a moving forest. But not so much as to lose each other." Jack replied.

"That will allow an easier time to break off into different directions when the time comes."

Jamie rode up and down the line of the caravan. "When we get out of the tunnels, each group must head towards any trees or forests they see, and quickly.' He shouted. 'Ash and Jonesy will take the lead; they know the way even better than I do. Ben and I will take turns riding drag. That is okay with you isn't it, Ben?"

"Jamie, it's a great idea. Though we won't be able to help with the poles to hold the netting."

"You are correct, and it's a good thing that most of the livestock is already on the land, or we'd be in a real pickle."

"That's for sure Jamie."

"Keep an eye on the cats and dogs' kids. We don't want any of them running off into the woods, or into another tunnel, and getting lost." Ben shouted as he rode down to take his place at the end of the caravan.

As bulky as the netting was, it eventually covered nearly everything, and everyone, even the horses, cows, sheep, and people, who were walking, the chickens were all in cages, in the buckboards. The men on horseback held makeshift poles to hold up the netting, three horses in front, three in the back, and multiple men on horses throughout the line of the caravan. Every person, animal, and wagon had to be covered by the netting if it is to do any good.

"Moving out," Ash shouted back.

The caravan moved slowly through the tunnels, even though the netting wasn't needed yet, the consensus was that everyone including the animals needed to get used to it before they were out in the open.

The smell of human and animal sweat was hard to deal with in the beginning, at least for those from the upper town. There were so many of the poor who had been unable to have proper baths in many a year under the canopies, added to humans, were the cows, pigs, sheep, and small animals, it was quite the mixture.

The caravan moved off in what seemed like a crawl to all. "I sure hope we can speed things up soon," Ash said quietly to Jamie before he left to move to the back of the caravan.

"Me too Ash." Was all Jamie said as he rode off toward the back of the caravan, talking to each man on horseback, "keep that pole a bit higher please, we don't want to spook the livestock."

"Yes sir, each said, grumbling a bit under their breaths. We will need to take a bit of a break here and there sir. These poles are heavy."

"Not to worry Bud, we do have men to spell you all, and you can do a bit of walking, and get your land legs back," Jamie replied with a tiny smirk. *It will do these guys a lot of good to get used to heavy work before we reach the settlements.*

"Walk, after all this work, WALK?" one of the men yelled.

"Keep the noise down back there, none of us has anything to go back to now, but death for being traitors to the others in our previous station in life."

Silence filled the air, as each thought long and hard about the outcome of getting caught, as the caravan crawled forward. *It appears that as people are getting the hang of holding the poles, keeping the livestock, and themselves under the netting their pace was picking up just a bit.* Jamie thought as he rode on. *I envy Ash, being in the lead has got to be a lot quieter, with less anger coming at one.* 'I should reach Ben soon, and we can take places, I'll enjoy riding drag for a while instead of circling the wagons and getting yelled at he said quietly to himself. *I'm tired of the constant complaints. I do*

hope they slow down soon. Maybe, when people
can get a little more rest?

"Hi Ben, how's it going?"

"Not bad Jamie, and with you?"

"There is a lot of grumbling, complaining, and
discontent in the caravan, especially by the so-
called upper class who are riding and holding the
poles. They weren't happy to hear they'd be
walking when they got spelled."

"I don't expect they would be. But perhaps after
we get out into the country and away from the city,
we can stop for a breather, it will all calm down."
Ben responded hopefully.

"Do hope you are right Ben, though we have many
days of traveling before that will happen."

"How many days do you think we have left till
then Jamie? Ben said as the rocks above him
shook. 'What was that?'

"I expect Nathan just blew the way into the
sewers.' Ben, as to how long, I'd say at least a few
days."

"That long? Do you think we can hold this mismatched group together without someone getting into a fight that long?"

"We have to Ben, but I do think they just might be too tired to fight, at least most of the time. grumble a bit, but not fight. With that, Jamie rode off, to the front of the caravan.

"Hey Ash, how's it going?"

"We absolutely must pick up speed Jamie or we won't make it out of the tunnels on time."

"I don't know how much more I can push these weary people, Ash."

"How about we tell them to pick up speed for an hour, and then they can rest, and eat for about half an hour? After that, they will need to push it for at least three or four hours before another break."

"That might work Ash, the thought of a break just might do it, though I do think I won't tell them that they will have to push hard for three or four hours before another break. At least, not until they have rested, and eaten."

"You know these people best Jamie."

CHAPTER NINETEEN

Grumbles could be heard down the line of the caravan of wagons. *I'm afraid it will soon become more than grumbling.* Jamie thought. *I need to talk to Ben and Ash about what we can do to calm things down and soon.*

As if on cue, Jamie could hear men yelling, and picked up speed toward it. "Stephen, what's happening?"

"I'm not used to all this walking Jamie. I shouldn't have to when this 'man' is up on the wagon riding. He's used to hard work, I'm not."

Ben, Ash, Carlos, and Smitty arrived just in time to hear Stephen and waited to hear how Jamie would handle the man who had been a friend in the upper town.

"Stephen we are all tired. Joshua spent the last six hours loading wagons and walking. We discussed this kind of attitude in the upper town years ago. If we hadn't, I'd throw you right off this caravan and have Smitty take you through the sewers and into the upper towns and leave you to fend for yourself up there. I can tell you they won't go easy on you.

What's more, you will not be able to give away where we are or where we are going.

It is no longer tolerated for anyone to hold themselves higher than another because of the color of their skin, their beliefs, the clothes they wear, or anything else, do you understand me now?"

"I'm sorry Jamie, and you to Joshua. We are all tired, but there was and is no excuse for my language or treatment of you, may I call you Joshua? Will you forgive me, and have patience with my lack of knowledge of others? I promise I will learn. Please call me Stephen. If you'd do me the honor, I'd like to invite you and your family to my campfire for supper tonight. Perhaps we can all get to know each other better."

"Yes, you can call me Joshua, Stephen, and it would be nice to come meet your family tonight."

"Jamie, I am sorry it won't happen again. We will learn to get to know others and hopefully become friends."

"I would like you to know that Joshua has a knack for machinery and can learn much from you and you from him."

"That will make for some interesting times together Joshua."

"Yes, I believe it will and my wife is a really good cook too."

"Thank you, Stephen, I hope you all have a good time tonight. I must tell you that we will not be able to stop long for supper. I'm told we must be out of the tunnels in a much shorter time than we expected

"How much time do we have Jamie?" Both men asked.

"A few days and that means every last one of us must be well out of the tunnels and into hiding."

"A few days? There are miles of tunnels to go through."

"Unfortunately, yes. But it must be done. That's all we have." Jamie answered.

Ben, Carlos, Ash, and Smitty watched as Jamie handled the problem. They might need to do the same soon.

"I'll see you two later. We stop in two hours for a meal break, and a bit of rest for everyone, especially those who have been walking."

"If you get a chance stop by our campfire and have a cuppa with us, Jamie?" Stephen stated as Jamie turned his horse to ride away.

"I'll try Stephen, if not tonight one night soon." He said as he rode off to meet with his fellow trail bosses.

As he reached Ben, Carlos, Ash, and Smitty he noticed they were watching Stephen and Joshua. He turned and looked. Joshua had gotten down off his wagon, leaving his wife to drive, and was walking next to Stephen talking.

As Jamie reached his friends, he said. "We need to have a conference tonight and it must be very private."

"Agreed!"

"Do you know what Jewell and Carolyn are doing?" Ben said.

"No what?"

"Well Jewell is teaching the women how to reach the between times, even during the daytime, and Carolyn is teaching the women and children to read."

"That is great Ben."

"Jamie, do you know if we have any teachers on the train that can begin to help the men learn to read and write?" Carlos asked.

"We do, Carlos, I will ask them to start. There will be times during our trek that a few can sit together in the wagons when they are not on walking duty." Jamie answered.

"I can help with that too," Ben spoke up.

As the day turned into night, the entire group began to get into a rhythm and started to make better time.

Even the ones holding the poles and shepherding the livestock were no longer complaining about the long hours and the muscles on their arms were getting stronger.

Riding up to Ben, Jamie said. "I do believe we'll be out of these tunnels quicker than the few days we were given."

"That will be good. What then Jamie, where do we go?"

"Tonight, when we stop, I'll tell you all," Jamie replied.

CHAPTER TWENTY

As Ben passed by the women's wagon, he felt a massing of a strange but beautiful power run through him, making the hairs on the back of his arms stand up.

"Jewell, I don't know that I can do it." Sarah piped up followed by a chorus of other women.

"I know it's hard to learn to pull in the magic of the between times even during the time when it's not yet day or night. But you've all felt the magic, you've all experienced the power. I know we can together pull it in even during the day to protect us all from those who will seek to find us and put us back into the slavery that was our lives. I know we can do this together."

"Are you sure? How do we even begin to start?"

"First, we learn how to become one with the universe and each other. Let's start by holding hands, closing our eyes, and just reaching out to feel the spirit of the one sitting next to you."

Looking at Jewell with doubt in their eyes, they each took the hand of the one next to them. "Now close your eyes and breathe," Jewell said.

The sweet scent of flowers long gone filled the air as the women breathed and connected to each other. The air filled with humming; a glow appeared on each face. They had touched the magic of the universe.

As they pulled it into themselves, shared as Jewell had told them they pictured a blue dome of light covering the entire three miles of the caravan. All felt a softness, a glowing, a sense of peace, happiness, hope, and safety.

There was not a man, woman, child, or animal who didn't feel the powerful force around them. Their steps picked up the pace a little as energy lit their souls.

Some whispered quietly to each other about seeing a blue haze appear and encircle the wagons.

"We did it, Sarah," Sarah said quietly. All the women were tired, and hungry, but energized at the same time.

"Yes, we did.' Jewell agreed. 'And we can easily reinforce it when needed. Do any of you know of any others that would be likely candidates to participate, we will need a steady stream of power going out to hide our progress as we move forward to our new homes. It is probable that we will not all stay together and as such, each of you will need to have your own circle."

"I will ask," Sarah said.

"Me too." The rest chimed in.

"Thank you.' Jewell said quietly. 'Now let us get some food and rest.

Jamie, Ben, Carlos, Ash, and Smitty all noticed the blue haze as well as the quietness that settled over the three-mile caravan. Looking at each other each smiled quietly. "That will help us," Jamie said.

"That's my daughter. I knew she could teach them."

"Will it be enough?" Ash asked.

"If they can sustain it, it should be. Most of us have seen what her tapestries can do. But I fear she will need to recruit many more women, and yes men too." Jamie added.

"For now, we are as safe as we can be, and I will tell you the plan. "As soon as we get out of the tunnels, we will be breaking up into five or six groups. Ash, Smitty, Carlos, Ben, Jonesy, and I will oversee one group each. We will stay as close to the abandoned buildings, trees, or whatever structures we can find as we move out of the area." Jamie stated to the group when they stopped for a brief rest.

"What will we do from their Jamie?"

"Ben, I have made maps of each group's routes, it will be a hard trip with few rest breaks. Each group will need to make twenty miles a day, and those walking will need to switch often with those that are riding. We will meet near Kenilworth Wisconsin; at that point, we should be far enough away to join up again for most of the duration to our destinations."

"Twenty miles is going to be rough to do Jamie, even trained walkers have trouble doing it."

"Yet if we are to get clear of those who will try to enslave or kill us, we will need to do it."

"Jamie, what is our final destination?" Ben asked.

"Hillsville South Dakota."

"That will take at least a couple of months Jamie."
Ash piped in.

"Probably a little over three months if we are lucky
Ash. Especially since we have about five thousand
people on this caravan. Luckily, I sent over five
thousand men, women, and children ahead to start
building more homes."

"Jamie, will they all be single-family homes?
Carlos asked.

"Not to start with, we won't have time for that. Not
all of the men are building, some are planting
crops. But most of the newer housing will be a
barrack style dwelling to give more people
protection from the coming winter."

"I suspect your planning is spot on Jamie. We will
need both food come spring and a place to house
everyone over the winter. It's early May now, if
we are lucky, we will all arrive by late August.
That will give us some time to put up more
housing, barns for the livestock, and buildings to
hold the seeds." Ben piped in.

"Ben, Ash, and I have been planning this for many
years now, we just didn't expect over ten-thousand
people. We have over five thousand between those
walking and those riding as it is."

"What other things do you believe we need to discuss before we call it a night?" Jamie said.

"Do you think we should pull together more men and women that can teach reading, writing, basics in agriculture, electronics, etc?" Smitty asked.

"That's a good idea. I'll put Carolyn and Stephen on it right away. Also, the women that Jewell has taught to use the magic to hide us, must pull together their own groups to teach the magic to. We won't all be living in the same town, and each town will need its individual protection." Jamie replied.

TWENTY-ONE

As the days went by the front of the caravan sighted the end of the sewer where it met the EL.

"Pass the word down the line, the front has arrived, and we need to have the entire wagon train out of the tunnels, split up into groups, the tunnel blown, and begin our separate treks until we arrive at our destination.' Ash yelled back to the man behind him. 'Tell each that tonight we must meet with the head of each wagon. Everyone must know what to do when we are out of the tunnels."

"Yo!" Said Smitty as he rode back to start passing the word.

The men on horseback and those walking began to spread the word down the line. Within half an hour the entire train of wagons had the word. Every man, woman, and child knew and started picking who would attend the meeting that night with the leaders of the caravan. Each was eager to be out of the tunnels and on their way. Though they all knew that more danger lurked ahead out in the open.

As night fell the group of men and women waiting for the beginning of the meeting grew. They whispered among themselves, each speculating on what was to come next.

"Shush!! They are coming."

Someone had started a fire and the women had begun to make coffee and warm up last night's stew. No one could afford to skip a meal, and all were already tired and hungry after a long day of traveling through the dark tunnels.

Jamie, with Jewell riding next to him, Ben with Carolyn, Ash, Smitty, and Carlos rode up and dismounted to a hushed crowd of people.

"Pass them some coffee.' Someone yelled, they probably need it."

"Thank you, we do!" said Jamie."

"I'm going to start this meeting by first getting information from you all. Stephen and Carolyn, how is the rounding up of teachers going?"

"Good, Jamie. Together we have about sixty or so that can teach various things, starting with the basics."

"That is great, they can then start teaching the others. Jewell, do you have enough women who can work the magic to keep us under cover and safe?"

"I've taught about thirty so far and they've started teaching others. I do believe they will make it by the time we split."

"What do you mean split?" Stephen cried out.

"We are going to need to split the caravan into smaller groups to avoid the chance of being caught," Ben stated flatly.

"Where do we go?"

"How will we find each other again?"

"Let's not get ahead of ourselves. First, we need men to build ramps to get the wagons and animals down to the ground. They must do it under the guise of night and do it quietly. We need volunteers that understand a bit about building."

A loud chorus of men shouted that they would volunteer. No one wished to stay any longer than necessary in the tunnels.

"I recommend those who know how to build or help carry supplies and water move into a separate group," Smitty said loudly.

As the crowd reshuffled and a large group of men split off the rest began unloading the wagon of nails, boards, strapping, planks, food, and water.

"Are five thousand already there Jamie?" Ben asked.

"Probably not all of them yet, I've been quietly moving people out for months now. But only a wagonload or two at a time and through the sewers. I couldn't take a chance of moving more than that at a time, not before now. A few thousand will be there working already, the rest will be there soon."

"Where did you find so many?" Stephen asked.

"Most from either the lower towns, and those that lost their jobs and were afraid they'd end up in the sewers, and a few from the upper town that were in a hurry to get started. Ash and I had to be careful about who we recruited." Jamie answered.

"How are we going to separate and where are we going?" A question came from the crowd.

"Most of what was once Evanston and Skokie were taken over by forest when the upper and lower towns were built. We will separate into the trees at that time according to Jonesy we should be just north of the city. That should be a good place for us to move out until we meet up in Kenilworth Wisconsin, just outside of Cedarburg. It's a much smaller town and it might not even be populated anymore. From there we will head out as one column to Eyota, Minnesota, which is over the halfway mark.' Jamie stated. 'Jonesy knows the area so his group will go first out and point out the direction for others to head in. He will also give you maps to help your group get to Kenilworth, where we will meet up again." Jamie said forcefully. 'We will still need to make twenty miles a day, and those walking will need to switch often with those that are riding."

"Twenty miles is going to be rough to do Jamie, even trained walkers have trouble doing it," Ash stated.

"Yet if we are to get clear of those who will try to enslave or kill us, we will need to do it," Jamie replied.

"Above all, we must avoid any human settlement. They probably will not be friendly." Jonesy stated firmly."

"Each group will be given a second map to follow should you miss us in Kenilworth. I warn you all it will take us a few months to get to our destination if all goes well, we should all be there by mid to late August."

"How many wagons per group?" Someone else asked.

"I'm figuring we can get away with about fifteen to twenty wagons per group. That's about five to six groups."

"Who's going to be in charge of each group of wagons?" Joshua spoke up.

"For the trip, since we know the routes best, Carlos, Ben, Smitty, Ash, Jonesy, and I will be the leaders of each section. We've memorized the maps to get there, but we should have backup men and women should something happen to one of us. Also, each group should pick a backup person to lead should something happen to the current leader."

As Jamie was speaking, the crowd began separating to allow a small group of men to come through.

TWENTY-TWO

Everyone turned around and watch as Nathan and about twenty men moved through the path toward the front.

A few of them were helping an injured man. All appeared exhausted, their clothes ripped and bloody. But still, they moved forward.

"Nathan, how did you find us, and what is happening in the upper town?' Ben asked. 'We haven't heard anything from above in days."

"Before they answer have a bit of pity Father. Let them eat, have some coffee, and let us treat the wounds of those that are hurt.' Jewell stated firmly. 'Do we have anyone qualified to treat these men?"

A small thin man and a woman approached the front. "I was a doctor in the upper town, and Simone a midwife in the lower town. We can help the injured."

"Thank you, what is your name?"

"Just call me doc most did." He said moving toward the injured men with Simone at his side.

"Mabel, and Sarah would you please help me get them some food and coffee?" Jewell asked politely.

"Of course, they said in unison." As they hurried to Jewell's side by the little campfire.

"A little warm water and soap over here please." OLyn hollered to the group in general.

Maria, Jonesy, and Stewart rushed over with a pail of water, a couple of dishes, soap, and towels.

As the small band of men cleaned up, ate a bit of food, and Doc and Simone treated the wounds of the injured, everyone stood watching.

Nathan was the first to start speaking, his mouth still crammed with food as he did so. "The upper town is in shambles. We blew up the ammunition centers, and the electric, and gas grids, and were able to get into the grid that controls the planes, drones, and tanks and destroy the computers that run them. It will buy some more time."

"That is good news Nathan, how did you find us?"

"I knew the only real way out of here was to get to the end of the subway. We followed how we could through the sewers but did run into a blue haze that screwed up our sight, but we were still able to track by using the sewer walls and our knowledge of them to get here. There is nothing else we can do in the upper town."

"What is happening up there now?" Ash asked.

"The government groups are fighting street to street with those from the lower towns. There is a lot of looting going on, though I have no idea what they will do with things like TV's. I don't think they do either."

"And the rich? Ben asked.

"Some have fled, some are in hiding, most have been killed by the looters."

"That is depressing, even though they were on the wrong side of history. It's still heartbreaking, some were greedy, others lazy, and many were just uninformed. Some of these people I knew." Jamie said quietly.

"At least we got their children out," Carolyn stated.

"That is true," Ash said.

Nathan continued. "The streets are very bloody. Lake Michigan is flooding the city, and the air has gotten very bad. We fought those who used to be known as the Oath Keepers, Proud Boys, QAnon, and Three Percenters in and out of buildings. I believe they are just about out of ammunition now. That's when we decided to leave and come find you all. There was nothing further we could accomplish there."

"You were right to leave Nathan. I don't believe there is anything further you could have done to help those that deserved and needed help." Jamie stated sadly.

Looking around at those listening Ben noticed his friend, Stephen, looking mournfully at Nathan.

"It was once such a beautiful city," Ben said looking at Stephen.

"Yes, it was, and I mourn for all that was lost and those that wouldn't listen to anyone. They were so sure of their superiority and the place they held. Intent on keeping only the luxury without any soul in them. At least none that I found when talking with them over the years. Still, it is so heartbreaking."

"That it is Stephen, I can even mourn the man I used to call father before I knew what he was as a man and a person. But enough of that for now, we will have many years to discuss the past. Today we have a future to seek."

"Agreed." Stephen said and everyone that remembered what Chicago had been, what the world once was nodded."

Just then Doc shouted, "Nathan please come here now."

Nathan went hurrying over to Doc. "What is it?"

"Your man here wants to speak to you and his time is short."

"You mean....?"

"Yes!!!"

Nathan squatted down next to one of his injured men. "What is it, Robert?"

"Did we buy them enough time Nathan?" Did we keep our oath to each other and them?"

"Yes, Robert we did. You shouldn't worry about that right now. Now is when you need all your energy to heal."

"We both know I'm not long for this world Nathan. Even Doc knows that. I just needed to know if we did right. If we did, I could rest easy, and die easy. I'll have made up for my wrongs."

"I believe with all of me, we bought them enough time to get away, to be far enough away that they will never be found, and they can rebuild a better world."

"Why did we believe all those lies? We were a part of those that helped bring about the horror that it all became?"

"We were young my friend and didn't know how to think yet. Forgive yourself as everyone here forgives you. We did well. You did great. Without you, we couldn't have bought all these people the time to get away."

With that, a small smile creased the corners of Robert's eyes just as his head fell to the side and he was gone.

A long sob went through the crowd as Nathan held his brother and friend in his arms weeping onto his shoulder. The others in his group hovered around him, grief hanging over all of them.

"Jamie is there a way we can bury him outside in the open air? He always missed the air, the trees, and the wind in his hair."

"We can take him with us into the forest and bury him properly in a place where he would have been happy. I hope one day you will tell us more about him?"

"When we are settled I will, he turned to his men, please help me carry him to one of the buckboards. Cover him as best you can so that he won't be harmed."

Still weeping they swept up Robert in their arms, following Jamie and Nathan to one of the buckboards that had once held building supplies but was emptier now. Laying him down gently, wiping his face with a cloth, they stood not yet ready to leave and unsure what else they could do to protect the body of their comrade when Jewell walked up carrying one of her precious tapestries. She placed it over his body, covering him from head to toe, with a gentleness in her hands.

"Thank you." Was all Nathan could say.

"You are welcome I would also like to hear his story one day, but for now I know he should be buried like a king."

"He was one of the best of us all," Nathan said, standing for a minute before turning back to Jamie.

"Thank you to sir, for I know what you are and what you stand for. My men and I beg you to join your caravan and help build a good world."

"Nathan I'd like to put you as second in command for one of the groups of wagons. We can fill you in later as to where we are going and how we will get there."

"Are you sure Jamie?" Nathan asked.

"You've earned it, and as a result, I believe you can be trusted. Plus, you have a way of surviving and bringing others through with you and you have empathy and love in your heart and soul despite all that you have been through. That is an important quality."

TWENTY-THREE

"Okay all, we best be getting our things together, eating a bite of food, feeding our families, and the livestock, and resting a bit. The men building the ramps up ahead should be finished in about another hour. At that time, we need to start moving out."

"Why didn't the men you sent months ago build those ramps?" Stephen asked.

"That is a good question and one everyone should hear the answer to.' Jamie replied. 'Please spread it up and down the line, that we couldn't take a chance that someone would see the ramps before now."

"I will and thank you."

After hearing what Jamie told Stephen, Adam asked. "Jamie, do you think we will have the last of the wagons out of the tunnels in another couple of hours?"

"Yes, I do believe we will, at that time each group must be ready to head into the forests in different directions."

"Jamie, Ash said, should we plan which group will go in which direction now?"

"No, I believe we can hold back and send them off in the correct direction as each group gets out of the tunnel, and not waste the time right now by trying to explain to them what they can't physically see."

"That makes sense."

"Jamie, you did right by Nathan and his men. Everyone is talking about how you and Jewell showed such compassion and leadership to those that once were our enemies yet became our trusted companions."

"Ash, I did nothing that you, Ben, Carlos, Smitty, or any of the others would have done."

"I'm not going to argue with you Jamie, but I know different. Remember I've known you all your life. You could have been so much different, just like your father or his ilk."

"Coming from you Ash that means much. Let us both go get something to eat before we start moving out. I need to talk to Jewell for a few minutes so if you will excuse me."

With a smile, Ash just nodded and walked off, as Jamie headed toward Jewell.

Taking her hand in his, he quietly said. "Can you spare me a few minutes?"

Smiling shyly, she nodded, knowing nearly everyone was watching them.

"What is it, Jamie?"

"I'd like you to stay with my group if your father approves. Would that be okay with you? I know we don't know each other very well, but I feel such a connection with you and somehow it is easier when you are around me."

A small smile lit her eyes as she nodded. *What is wrong with me that I can't seem to think of a thing to say when he is around?* She thought.

"I'll ask him now if that suits you?"

"It does Jamie." She felt as if her face was on fire, and the touch of his hand nearly burned her skin with a strange sensation of passion building. *This has never happened to me before, not even when I worked in the Between Times did, I feel such a sense of connection with another person.*

"Soon it will be dusk Jewell, and we will need to lead the first wagons out of the tunnels. But first I need to tell you that I know you are too young for me."

Jewell interrupted. "No Jamie don't say it. What will be is what is right. Remember what Rebecca said and there was as much of an age difference between her and my father. Whatever is between us will sort itself out as time goes by."

Quietly they moved off to get something to eat and get some rest before they began to check on the status of every single person in the caravan.

"We need to go have a conference with the ones who will be leading each group and update everyone."

"Agreed."

Ben and Carolyn looked up with a smile watching Jewell and Jamie coming toward them holding hands.

Sitting down in front of the small campfire, all was quiet as Maria passed out food and coffee to Jamie and Jewell. Everyone else already had theirs.

"So, who is leading which group?" Jonesy asked, pretending to ignore the fire he saw passing between Jewell and Jamie.

"Jewell where are we on teaching how to control the between times that will keep each group safe?"

"I've trained about seven groups of those Carolyn, Mabel, Sarah, Maria, Joshua's wife Anita, and Stephen's wife Joanna are the best and can lead a circle by themselves."

Carolyn and Maria blushed, as Jamie said. "Well, that makes sense if you think about it, each of them has some of the old blood in them, and it makes it easier to break up the groups."

"Who is going first?" Ben asked.

"Jonesy knows the area best so he should go first. We'll put Mable and Jacob in Jonesy's group. He'll be able to direct the different groups for the initial split up."

"That makes sense.' Ash stated. 'Who's next?"

"You will be Ash, with Stephen and Joanna in your group. Then Ben and Carolyn."

"Wait what about Jewell coming with me?" Ben asked.

"Jewell will be riding with me. We will bring up the back just behind Smitty, and make sure all is clear behind us. She is the most powerful with using the between times and can keep the back clear of any looking for us." Jamie stated.

"That worries me, Jamie."

"I'm sure it would worry me too Ben, but I need her with me, and that is where she belongs."

"Who's next?" Carlos called out.

"You and Maria, followed by Joshua and Anita's group, then Jewell and I will be behind Sarah and Smitty. Smitty will need to blow up the exit after everyone is out."

"Where will Nathan's group be?" Smitty asked.

"With you Smitty in case you need help. You okay with that?"

"Yo!"

"If it's okay with you Nathan, we will wait and bury Robert in Kenilworth when we all meet up again!"

"I'd like that," Nathan said mournfully.

"Any other questions or concerns?" Jamie asked.

"I'm still not happy with Jewell being so far back and away from me," Ben said.

"It must be this way, Ben. We must have an order and that must be the order we need to make sure we all get through, and all have protection, direction."

"I guess there is a reason for it all Jamie, I'm just unused to Jewell not being with me is all, and it will be months before I see her again and make sure she is okay."

"I promise you I will keep her safe Ben. But I do understand your worry. I feel pretty much the same about OLyn, being so far away for so long."

"Oh look!!! Jewell cried.

Everyone turned around and looked off into the distance.

Lo and behold you could see Sable leading a pack of older cats and dogs through the caravan. At each wagon, a dog or cat would break from the rest and hop aboard a wagon.

Everyone smiled at the sight. "Sable didn't forget the older ones; they need safety and homes too," Jewell stated happily.

TWENTY-FOUR

As they began to move out of the sewers and onto
the old EL stop at the Howard Street station, each
group of wagons climbed the ramps up and then
down onto what was left of the streets below. Like
clockwork they split off in the direction they were
told to go, moving quickly behind broken-down
buildings, into the forest that had taken over the
town in those fifteen years since the divide of the
rich from the poor happened.

There was silence among them, and a blue haze of
protection could be seen covering the movement of
each group as it moved off. It would be weeks
before they met up again to become one caravan of
people moving together toward a new hope.

By the time the last of the wagons and people had
left the tunnels they were already filling with water
from the flooding that happened when the outer
walls around Chicago were breached, and Lake
Michigan began flooding the city.

Still, if one looked you could almost see the last of
the tallest buildings in what had been one of the
greatest cities in the country.

Jamie wondered what would be left of it. *I believe I will ask Nathan what he saw last when I get the chance.*

"You are so far away Jamie, what are you thinking of?" Jewell asked putting her hand on his.

"Chicago, what was and what is now happening. But enough of that for now. I've decided you must also teach me how to control the Between Times Jewell. That is if you think I can and are willing?"

"You have the Celtic blood, Jamie; you can learn and yes I will teach you."

The simple touch of her hand on his sent fire through them both.

God, I don't know how long I will be able to keep my hands and lips off her. Jamie thought.

It is so hard not to pull him to me, to touch him, to love him. Yet I know it is not yet time. There is so much we have yet to do and to learn about each other, and we must get to the end of this journey safely too."

Jamie looked back, they were now miles away from Chicago, yet far off in the distance, he thought he could see drones flying. Oh, not a lot of them, but still a few. They didn't seem to be coming closer though and that was a good sign. His group could no longer see any of the others. With luck, everyone will make it safely to Kenilworth where we will meet up, from there it will be a long trek, but we will have each other for company and know we are probably safe from any attacks from the city.

We will still need to watch out for those who escaped the Divide and live in hiding in the forests, and small towns. But still, we will be safer at that point in numbers, and we have the power of the Between Times.

"What will happen when we reach our destination, Jamie?"

"We will build a new world. One free of hate, and without a need to treat others as less, with luck there will no longer be a need to put others down to feel better about themselves."

"It sounds too good to be true Jamie."

"Oh, there will be those that will accrue more money, that live in better houses, but hopefully we can teach each other and the children that money and status doesn't make a difference in the person. But instead, it just makes them want to give a helping hand to those in need or those who wish to better their lives. That is my hope."

"Mine too Jamie." Jewell said gazing at him with a heart full of admiration and love.' And we will see what our future together will be."

"Yes, dear heart. We will see, perhaps we will even know before this trip is over."

"I believe we will at that Jamie."

I have seen our babies, though have not told him yet. They will not be born before we arrive, but there will be many, and Father and Carolyn will have children too. Jewell thought as the wagon moved on toward Kenilworth.